A FEATHER, A PEBBLE, A SHELL

TO MY PARENTS, WHOSE LOVE OF NATURE HAS ALWAYS INSPIRED ME

KAR-BEN PUBLISHING®
An imprint of Lerner Publishing Group, Inc.
241 First Avenue North
Minneapolis, MN 55401 USA
Website address: www.karben.com

Photos on page 31 are provided by the author.

Main body text set in Imperfect OT Regular.
Typeface provided by T-26.

Library of Congress Cataloging-in-Publication Data

Names: Leshem-Pelly, Miri, author. | Leshem-Pelly, Miri, illustrator.
Title: A feather, a pebble, a shell / author and illustrator Miri Leshem-Pelly.
Description: Minneapolis, MN : Kar-Ben Publishing, An imprint of Lerner Publishing Group, Inc., [2024] | Audience: Ages 3–8 | Audience: Grades K–1 | Summary: "When the Israeli author-illustrator runs in a field or swim in the sea, she looks for something to hold in her hand: a pebble or a feather. She leaves them in their habitats...for the reader to find"— Provided by publisher.
Identifiers: LCCN 2023004433 (print) | LCCN 2023004434 (ebook) | ISBN 9798765607749 (library binding) | ISBN 9798765613399 (epub)
Subjects: LCSH: Ecology—Juvenile literature. | Habitat (Ecology)—Juvenile literature.
Classification: LCC QH541.14 .L4725 2024 (print) | LCC QH541.14 (ebook) | DDC 577—dc23/eng/20230530

LC record available at https://lccn.loc.gov/2023004433
LC ebook record available at https://lccn.loc.gov/2023004434

Manufactured in China
1-1010309-52378-10/24/2023

0724/B2543/A5

A FEATHER, a PEBBLE, a SHELL

MIRI LESHEM-PELLY

KAR-BEN
PUBLISHING

Whenever I run in an open field,
climb up a hill,
or swim in the sea,

I look for something small to hold in my hand.

I crouch on a warm boulder in the Dan River,
where clear water burbles over pebbles.

I reach for one of the round,
black pebbles,
but oh!
The water is ice cold.

I leave the pebble
lying in its riverbed.

BASALT PEBBLE
This rock was formed from lava
over one hundred thousand
years ago, when volcanoes
were active in the area. The
rapidly cooling lava contained
bubbling gases that caused
many holes to form in the rocks.

Along a narrow trail
on Mount Meron,

I step on rocks, on roots, on crunchy leaves,
where a porcupine strolled the night before

and left a pointed gift.

QUILL OF AN INDIAN CRESTED PORCUPINE
Porcupine quills are made of stiff hair. The longest quills can reach up to 20 inches (51 cm).

A wave chases me on the sand of Dor Beach.
I'm caught!

Closer . . . closer . . .

Clear water slowly recedes,
gliding over rattling seashells,
leaving my bare feet alone.

SHELL OF A VIOLET BITTERSWEET CLAM

The violet bittersweet clam species has been extinct for one thousand years. This shell is probably even older.

In the Sharon Nature Reserve,
I can smell the wetness of the earth.
Raindrops tap on sleepy snails,
crowded on a flower stem.

They wake up,
stretch their tentacles,
and get ready for their winter feast.

But on the ground one empty
shell is left behind.

I hold it in my hand.

SHELL OF A
MEDITERRANEAN SNAIL
When this snail goes into a long
sleep during the hot summer,
predators—such as beetles,
spiders, and mice—can easily
catch and eat it, leaving
behind an empty shell.

I spot a hoopoe in the grass at HaYarkon Park.
Its long beak searches in the ground.

Peck, peck, peck. A caterpillar.
Peck, peck, peck. A worm.

Peck. A beetle. *Peck.* A cricket.
Hoopoe finds them all.

Suddenly the hoopoe spreads out
its feathered crown
and flies away.

FEATHER OF A HOOPOE
The feather crest on the hoopoe's
head is usually closed, but it spreads
open when the hoopoe is excited.
The hoopoe is Israel's national bird.

My fingers touch the wrinkled trunk of
an ancient tree in an orchard in Sataf.

But then, one small fruit—an olive—
falls and rolls on the ground,
as if the tree is telling me,
I'm old . . . but I'm alive.

FRUIT OF EUROPEAN OLIVE
Some olive trees can live more than one
thousand years. Based on its size, this olive
tree is probably about five hundred years
old. The olive tree is Israel's national tree.

Underground, inside the dark
Twins Cave in the Judaean Hills,

I hear water tap.

My flashlight reveals stalactites and stalagmites shaped like castle towers.

An underground kingdom.

STALACTITE
When water travels through the ground and drips down from the cave ceiling, it leaves calcium particles behind. Slowly, the particles accumulate to make a stalactite.

Bright sunlight makes me close my eyes
as I float weightless in the Dead Sea.

There are no seashells on the beach,
and no fish swim under me in the salty water.

Only salt crystals
that sparkle in the sun.

SALT CRYSTAL
The Dead Sea is really a lake, located in
the desert. The sun and the heat cause
the lake's water to evaporate, leaving a
high concentration of salt and minerals.

I look up above the canyon walls in Ein Avdat.
There, in a light blue strip of sky,
a giant griffon vulture is circling.

A long, dark feather
falls on the soft soil.

I pick it up and hold it high.

As I run, the feather surfs on air.
We soar.

FEATHER OF A GRIFFON VULTURE
The wingspan of the griffon vulture can reach 100 inches (254 cm). These vultures are native to Israel and nest in high rocky cliffs, such as the canyon walls of Ein Avdat.

An ibex climbs down the steep slope of a mountain in Barak Gorge.

I hide behind a big rock and watch.

His strong horns crash into the tree's thorny branch.
Again and again.

Finally, he bites the
long curvy pod of the
twisted acacia tree.

POD OF A TWISTED ACACIA TREE
Nubian ibexes love eating the fruit of this
tree. The tree benefits too. Acacia seeds that
have passed through the ibex's stomach
have a better chance of sprouting than
those that just fall to the ground.

I snorkel in the blue, blue world of the Red Sea,
where the only sound is my breath.

Fish play hide-and-seek
in their coral garden.

I raise my head above the water
to a world of loud sound,
dazzling light,
and desert heat,

while my feet dangle over
the calm coral reef.

DEAD HOOD CORAL

Each piece of coral is a colony
of thousands of small animals
called polyps. Baby polyps are
carried by the sea currents until
they land on a stony skeleton
of dead coral. They attach
themselves to the dead coral
and build the coral reef.

Whenever I hold something small in my hand—
a feather, a pebble, a shell—

I leave it where it belongs . . .

for you to find.

AUTHOR'S NOTE

Israel is a small country, similar in size to the state of New Jersey, yet its natural landscape is surprisingly diverse. Why is this so?

Geographic Location

Israel is a meeting point of three continents: Asia, Africa, and Europe. It borders both the Mediterranean Sea and the Red Sea. In Israel, you can find plants and animals typical to each of these different continents and seas.

Topographic Diversity

There are substantial elevation differences in Israel, from the high mountains of the Golan in the north to the Dead Sea valley, the lowest place on Earth.

Geological Diversity

Israel's earth is made up of several different rock and soil types. For example, there are areas of hard basalt rock and also areas of soft sand soil.

Climate Diversity

Israel has several different climate zones, ranging from the cold of snowy mountains in the north to the heat of arid deserts in the south. These varying conditions create the unusual range of landscapes, as well as a remarkable variety of plant and animal species.

This book is based on my personal experiences growing up as an Israeli in a family of nature lovers. We often hiked the country, and this book follows some of the geographic locations, from north to south, that we explored.

—Miri Leshem-Pelly

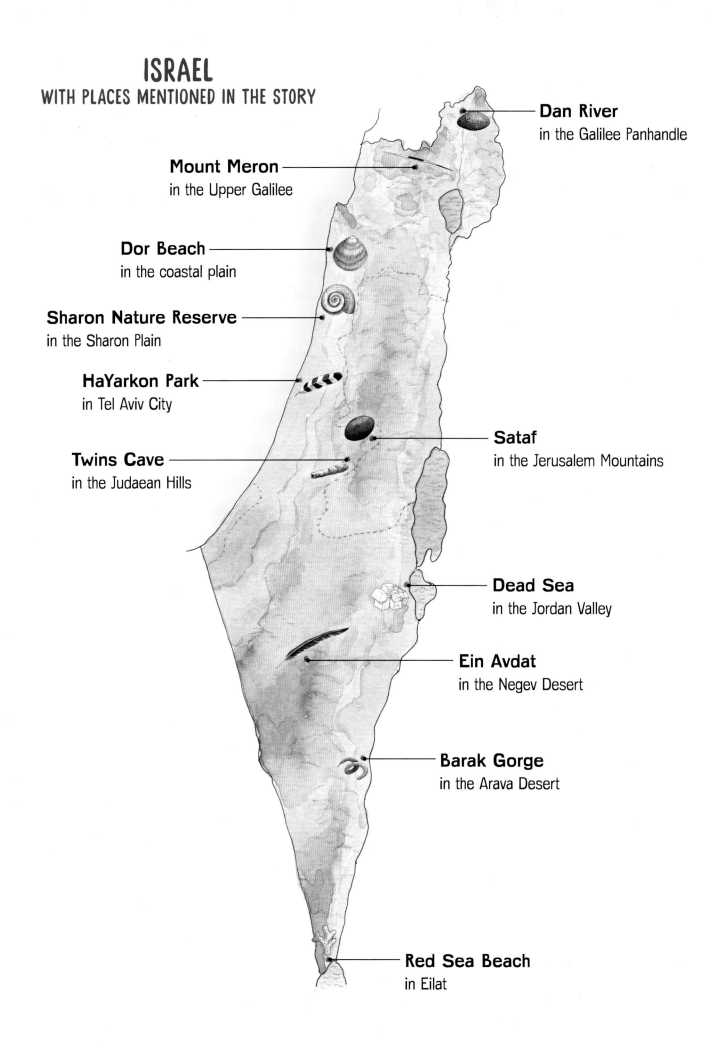

ISRAEL
WITH PLACES MENTIONED IN THE STORY

Dan River
in the Galilee Panhandle

Mount Meron
in the Upper Galilee

Dor Beach
in the coastal plain

Sharon Nature Reserve
in the Sharon Plain

HaYarkon Park
in Tel Aviv City

Sataf
in the Jerusalem Mountains

Twins Cave
in the Judaean Hills

Dead Sea
in the Jordan Valley

Ein Avdat
in the Negev Desert

Barak Gorge
in the Arava Desert

Red Sea Beach
in Eilat